LITTLE D
and the Ne

by Stephanie Calmenson

illustrated by
Kathy Cruickshank

A GOLDEN BOOK • NEW YORK

Western Publishing Company, Inc., Racine, Wisconsin 53404

© 1988 by Stephanie Calmenson. Illustrations © 1988 by Kathy Cruickshank. All rights reserved.
GOLDEN®, GOLDEN & DESIGN®, and A FIRST LITTLE GOLDEN BOOK® are trademarks of
Western Publishing Company, Inc. No part of this book may be reproduced or copied in any form
without written permission from the publisher. Library of Congress Catalog Card Number:
87-82391 ISBN: 0-307-10172-X   MCMXCI

Little Duck had a new baby sister.

"Waa! Waa!" cried Baby.

"I think she's hungry," said Little Duck.

"I think you're right," said Mommy.

While Mrs. Duck fed the baby, Little Duck fed his bear.

"Would you like to burp the baby?" asked Mrs. Duck when Baby finished her bottle.

Little Duck patted Baby on the back the way his mommy had taught him.

"Urp!" went Baby.

"Good job!" said Mrs. Duck.

"Now it's Bear's turn," said Little Duck.
Mrs. Duck patted Bear on the back.
"Urp!" went Bear.
"Uncle Mallard will be here soon," said
Little Duck's mommy. "Why don't you go
and wash while I dress Baby."

Little Duck was excited about seeing Uncle Mallard. They always had such a good time together. Little Duck practiced the song he wanted to sing for his uncle.

"Six little ducks that I once knew,
Fat ones, skinny ones, fair ones, too..."

"Don't dawdle, Little Duck," called Mommy.

Little Duck washed and sang faster:

"Down to the river they would go.
Wibble, wobble, wibble, wobble, to and fro."

Dingdong!
"Uncle Mallard is here!" called Mrs. Duck.
Little Duck finished washing, then ran to greet his uncle.

Daddy had already let Uncle Mallard in. Uncle Mallard was bending over Baby's cradle and didn't even notice when Little Duck came into the room.

"So you're my new niece!" said Uncle Mallard. "Kitchy-kitchy-coo! You're the cutest baby!"

"Hello, Uncle Mallard," said Little Duck. "Wasn't I cute, too?"

"Of course you were cute," he said. "And you still are!"

"I know a song," said Little Duck. "Do you want to hear it?"

"I'd love to hear your song," said Uncle Mallard. "But right now I want to visit with your new baby sister."

The next thing Little Duck knew, Uncle
Mallard was taking a big pink box from his
bag. It was a present for Baby!

Before the baby came, Uncle Mallard had
brought presents for Little Duck. But this
time Little Duck did not see anything for him.

"Uncle Mallard forgot all about me,"
Little Duck thought.

Little Duck was so upset, he ran to his room. "Baby! Baby! I *hate* the baby!" he shouted.

Little Duck's mommy went to his room and held him close. "Having a new baby around is hard sometimes," she said. "But you're still our special Little Duck, and we love you very much."

"Uncle Mallard loves you very much,
too," said Daddy, coming into the room.
"Why don't we go see what he's doing?"

They went into the living room. Uncle Mallard was looking at a picture album. And he was smiling.

"Isn't this a picture of you tumbling over?" said Uncle Mallard.

"That's me!" said Little Duck. Then he tumbled over and over right into Uncle Mallard's arms for a big hug.

"Would you like to see your present now?"
said Uncle Mallard, reaching into his bag.

"You didn't forget me!" said Little Duck.

"Of course not," said Uncle Mallard.

Little Duck tore the paper off his present.
It was a squirrel cup with a striped straw.

"Can I have juice in my new cup, Mommy?"

While Little Duck and his mommy were filling the cup, they heard a familiar sound.

"Waa! Waa!" cried Baby.

"Baby must be hungry again," said Mrs. Duck. "I'll get her bottle."

In the nursery Uncle Mallard tried to make Baby smile.

"Kitchy-kitchy-coo!" he said.

"Waa!" cried Baby.

Uncle Mallard made a funny face to make the baby laugh.

"Waa! Waa!" cried Baby, louder than before.

Little Duck came into the room. He leaned over Baby's crib and began to sing:

"Six little ducks that I once knew,
Fat ones, skinny ones, fair ones, too."

Baby looked at Little Duck and stopped crying.

Little Duck sang some more:

*"Down to the river they would go,
Wibble, wobble, wibble, wobble, to and fro."*

"Coo, coo, coo," said Baby.
"That's a fine song," said Uncle Mallard.
"And you are a wonderful big brother."

That night, when Little Duck's mommy
and daddy were tucking him in, Mommy said,
"Baby is lucky to have a big brother like you."
"I know," said Little Duck.

And he hummed himself to sleep.